RUBY'S NEW HOME

by **Tony** and **Lauren Dungy**

illustrated by

Vanessa Brantley Newton

Ready-to-Read

SCHOLASTIC INC.
New York Toronto London Auckland
Sydney Mexico City New Delhi Hong Kong

To our children: Tiara, James, Eric, Jordan, Jade, Justin, and Jason —T. D. and L. D.

"And do not forget to do good and to share with others, for with such sacrifices God is pleased."
—Hebrews 13:16 (NIV)

ISBN 978-0-545-49862-3

Text copyright © 2011 by Tony Dungy and Lauren Dungy.
Illustrations copyright © 2011 by Vanessa Brantley Newton.
Published in association with the literary agency of Legacy, LLC, Winter Park, FL 32789. All rights reserved. Published by Scholastic Inc., 557 Broadway, New York, NY 10012, by arrangement with Simon & Schuster Books for Young Readers, an imprint of Simon & Schuster Children's Publishing Division. SIMON SPOTLIGHT, READY-TO-READ, and colophon are registered trademarks of Simon & Schuster, Inc. SCHOLASTIC and associated logos are trademarks and/or registered trademarks of Scholastic Inc.

12 11 10 9 8 7 6 5 4 3 2 1   12 13 14 15 16 17/0

Printed in the U.S.A.   40

First Scholastic printing, September 2012

Everyone was excited!
Mom and Dad had a big surprise.
Today was the day Ruby would
arrive. The kids could not wait to
meet their new dog.

After lunch Mom and Dad brought Ruby home. "Everyone has to learn to share," Mom said. "We will all have to take care of Ruby."

"Isn't she cute?" Jade said.
"Ruby is going to be so much fun,"
said Jordan.
Justin smiled and nodded.
Everyone loved Ruby right away!

Mom took them to the pet store. She told each of them they could pick out something special for Ruby.

Jade picked out a leash
and bowl.

Jordan picked out a ball and blanket.
Justin picked out a collar and a tag.
Then he picked out a box of treats
for Ruby. Everything was red!
"Why did you all pick red?"
asked Mom.

"Her name is Ruby," said Jade.
"So red is her favorite color!"
Mom smiled. "I am glad we are
all sharing Ruby
so well," she said.

That night Mom heard loud voices. She walked down the hall to see what was going on. Justin was hugging Ruby.

Jordan was holding her ball.
And Jade was trying to pull Ruby
with her leash!

"What is going on here?" asked
Mom.

Jordan said, "Ruby is *my* dog.
I want her to sleep in my room."

Justin said, "No, Ruby is my dog.
I want her to sleep in my room."

Jade said, "Mom, they are both wrong. Ruby is my dog, and she should sleep in my room."

Just then Ruby barked.
They all let go of Ruby and looked
at Mom.

"Ruby is a member of our family,"
Mom said. "We need to share her.
There is plenty of fun to go around.
Ruby loves all of you. Right, Ruby?"

Everyone looked around. "Where is Ruby now?" asked Justin. Where did Ruby go? She was nowhere in sight!

They looked in Jordan's room.
No Ruby.

They looked in Jade's room.
No Ruby.

They looked in Justin's room.
No Ruby!

Then they looked downstairs.

Ruby was curled up in her crate
on her brand-new red blanket!
She was fast asleep.
"It looks like Ruby has found
her own spot to sleep," said Mom.

The next morning Dad
had a good idea.
"Let's have a picnic
at the park," he said.

"Can Ruby come too?" asked Jade.
"We can all play with her together!"
"I will bring Ruby's leash,"
said Justin.

"I will bring her ball," said Jordan.

"And I will bring her treats," said Jade.

They all took turns playing with Ruby. They all threw the ball for her to chase.

They took turns holding the leash
to keep her safely near them.
They all gave her treats
but not too many!

On the drive home Ruby fell
asleep in the back seat.
She was so tired she was snoring!

"Look, Mom," said Justin.
"Sweet little Ruby really is our
dog!"
Mom smiled. "Isn't sharing fun? We
can share taking care of Ruby, and
share playing with Ruby."

"Best of all," said Dad,
"we can share Ruby's love, too!"

READING ★ WITH ★ THE ★ STARS!

Simon Spotlight Ready-to-Read books showcase your favorite characters—the stars of these stories!

At every level, you are a reading star!

PRE-LEVEL ONE ★ RISING STAR READER!
Shared reading ★ Familiar characters ★ Simple words

LEVEL ONE ★ STAR READER!
Easy sight words and words to sound out ★ Simple plot and dialogue
Familiar topics and themes

LEVEL TWO ★ SUPERSTAR READER!
Longer sentences ★ Simple chapters ★ High-interest vocabulary words

LEVEL THREE ★ MEGASTAR READER!
Longer, more complex story plot and character development
Challenging vocabulary words ★ More difficult sentence structure

When Mom and Dad bring home a new puppy, everyone is so excited! All the kids love Ruby. But who gets to walk Ruby? Who gets to brush Ruby? Who gets to play with Ruby? Everyone needs to learn how to share their new best friend!

by Tony and Lauren Dungy   illustrated by Vanessa Brantley Newton

ISBN 978-0-545-49874-6

$3.99 US

50399

EAN

9 780545 498746